For Christopher Melling
Thanks Dad

JUST LIKE MY DAD
by David Melling

First published in the UK
© 2002 by Hodder Children's Books

This 2008 edition published by Sandy Creek,
by arrangement with Hodder Children's Books.

Sandy Creek
122 Fifth Avenue
New York, NY 10011

ISBN-13: 978 1 4351 1418 0

A catalogue record of this book is available from the British Library.

Printed and bound in China

1 3 5 7 9 10 8 6 4 2

Just Like My Dad

David Melling

SANDY CREEK

This is my dad.

One day, I'll have sharp teeth…

…just like my dad.

And spiky hair…

…just like my dad.

I'll grow long nails and a swishy tail…

...just like my dad.

and lick my nose…

...just like my dad.

When I eat my tummy talks...

gurgle

gurgle

…just like my dad's.

And when I lie around being
lazy, my mom says…

My dad says
I must not be
afraid of
anything...

big...

...or small.

Sometimes my dad can be a little cranky…

...but I can make him laugh really loud.

When we play
hide-and-seek with my
friends my dad likes
to go first...

But he's not very good!

Even so, all my friends say,
when they grow up they want to be...

...just like my dad.